THE CAT'S PAJAMAS

To librarians, parents, and teachers:

The Cat's Pajamas is a Parents Magazine READ ALOUD Original — one title in a series of colorfully illustrated and fun-to-read stories that young readers will be sure to come back to time and time again.

Now, in this special school and library edition of *The Cat's Pajamas*, adults have an even greater opportunity to increase children's responsiveness to reading and learning — and to have fun every step of the way.

When you finish this story, check the special section at the back of the book. There you will find games, projects, things to talk about, and other educational activities designed to make reading enjoyable by giving children and adults a chance to play together, work together, and talk over the story they have just read.

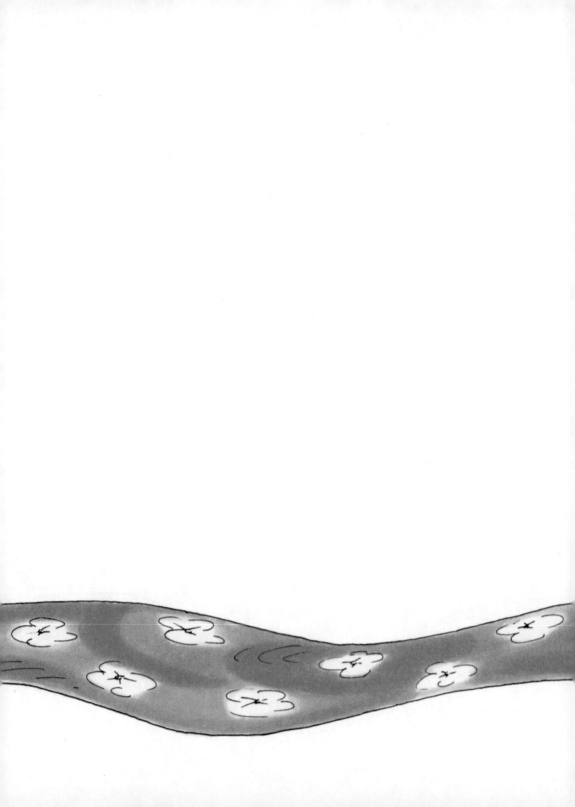

THE
CAT'S PAJAMAS

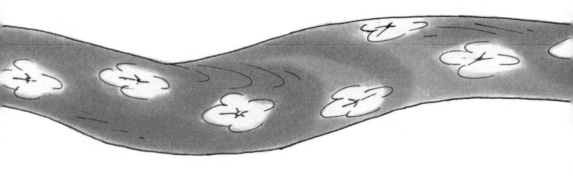

For a free color catalog describing Gareth Stevens' list of high-quality books, call 1-800-542-2595 (USA) or 1-800-461-9120 (Canada). Gareth Stevens' Fax: (414) 225-0377.

Parents Magazine READ ALOUD Originals:

A Garden for Miss Mouse
Aren't You Forgetting
   Something, Fiona?
Bicycle Bear
Bicycle Bear Rides Again
The Biggest Shadow in
   the Zoo
Bread and Honey
Buggly Bear's Hiccup Cure
But No Elephants
Cats! Cats! Cats!
The Cat's Pajamas
Clara Joins the Circus
The Clown-Arounds
The Clown-Arounds Go
   on Vacation
The Clown-Arounds Have
   a Party
Elephant Goes to School
The Fox with Cold Feet
Get Well, Clown-Arounds!
The Ghost in Dobbs Diner
The Giggle Book
The Goat Parade

Golly Gump Swallowed a Fly
Henry Babysits
Henry Goes West
Henry's Awful Mistake
Henry's Important Date
The Housekeeper's Dog
I'd Like to Be
The Little Witch Sisters
The Man Who Cooked
   for Himself
Milk and Cookies
Miss Mopp's Lucky Day
No Carrots for Harry!
Oh, So Silly!
The Old Man and the
   Afternoon Cat
One Little Monkey
The Peace-and-Quiet Diner
The Perfect Ride
Pets I Wouldn't Pick
Pickle Things
Pigs in the House
Rabbit's New Rug
Rupert, Polly, and Daisy

Sand Cake
Septimus Bean and His
   Amazing Machine
Sheldon's Lunch
Sherlock Chick and the
   Giant Egg Mystery
Sherlock Chick's First Case
The Silly Tail Book
Snow Lion
Socks for Supper
Sweet Dreams,
   Clown-Arounds!
Ten Furry Monsters
There's No Place Like Home
This Farm is a Mess
Those Terrible Toy-Breakers
Up Goes Mr. Downs
The Very Bumpy Bus Ride
Where's Rufus?
Who Put the Pepper in
   the Pot?
Witches Four

Library of Congress Cataloging-in-Publication Data

Chittum, Ida.
   The cat's pajamas / by Ida Chittum ; pictures by Art Cumings.
      p. cm. -- (Parents magazine read aloud original)
   Summary: Fred spends a lot of time and effort making his cat a pair of pajamas, but the cat won't wear them.
   ISBN 0-8368-1124-0
   [1. Cats--Fiction. 2. Clothing and dress--Fiction.] I. Cumings, Art, ill. II. Title. III. Series.
PZ7.C4453Cat 1995
[E]--dc20   94-35194

This North American library edition published in 1995 by Gareth Stevens Publishing, 1555 North RiverCenter Drive, Suite 201, Milwaukee, Wisconsin, 53212, USA, under an arrangement with Gruner + Jahr USA Publishing.

Text © 1980 by Ida Chittum. Illustrations © 1980 by Art Cumings. Portions of end matter adapted from material first published in the newsletter *From Parents to Parents* by the Parents Magazine Read Aloud Book Club, © 1990 by Gruner + Jahr USA Publishing, New York; other portions © 1995 by Gareth Stevens, Inc.

Printed in the United States of America

1 2 3 4 5 6 7 8 9 99 98 97 96 95

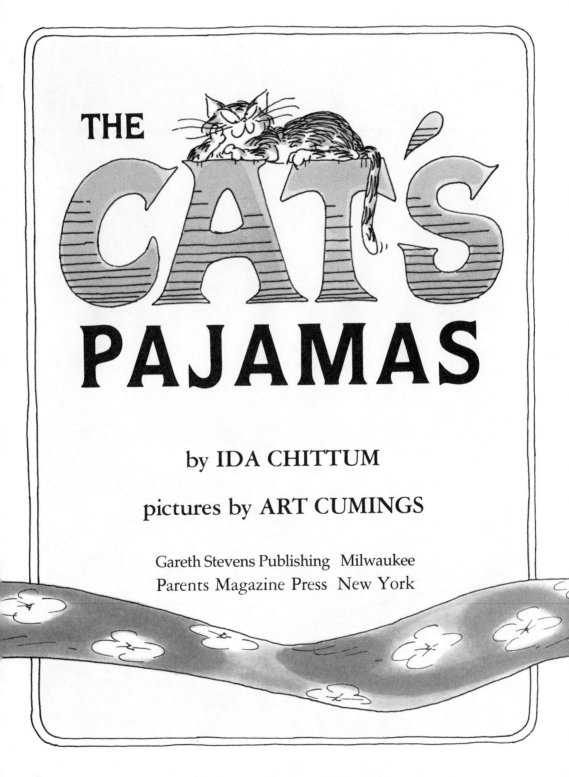

THE CAT'S PAJAMAS

by IDA CHITTUM

pictures by ART CUMINGS

Gareth Stevens Publishing Milwaukee
Parents Magazine Press New York

To eight cats I know:
Arthur, Molly, Max, Liddy,
Nelson, Mouse, Bugs, and Pip...
and to Poo'Chi Kou

The cat's pajamas started out as a big piece of red cloth with white flowers.

Fred folded the red cloth double
and laid it on the floor.
He placed the cat on the cloth
and drew around her.
He took the scissors
and cut out the cloth
around the crayon line.

Fred held up the two pieces of
red cloth with white flowers.
He said to Red, his dog,
"These are just right for
the cat's pajamas. All I
need is a nice long piece of
red thread to sew them together."

He looked in the sewing box.
He found yellow thread.
He found green thread.
But he couldn't find any red thread.

"Would you like to go with me?"
Fred said to Red.
"I am going over to Mr. May's house
to borrow a piece of red thread."
"Arf, arf!" Red said.

Fred knocked on the door.

Mr. May opened it.

"Hello," Fred said.

He held up the two pieces of cloth.

"These are the cat's pajamas.

All I need is a piece of red thread

to sew them together."

"One second, Fred," Mr. May said.
He went into the next room.
Fred heard Mr. May opening
and closing drawers.
He heard something fall
and hit Mr. May.

THUMP

Mr. May came out limping.
He said, "Sorry, Fred.
I couldn't find any red thread.
Why not try the family next door."
"Thank you," Fred said.

Fred and Red went next door.
Fred knocked. "Hello," he said.
He held up the two pieces of cloth.
"These are the cat's pajamas.
All I need is a nice long piece
of red thread to sew them together."

The woman at the door shook her head.
She hadn't heard a word Fred said.
Lots of little children behind her
were yelling all at once.
And a baby was kicking its feet and crying.
Fred decided that this was not a good place
to find a piece of red thread.

So he and Red went to the park.
A lady was sitting there with
her poodle and her sewing basket.
"Hello," Fred said.
He held up the two pieces of
red cloth with white flowers.
"These are the cat's pajamas.
All I need is a nice long piece of
red thread to sew them together."

The lady reached into her sewing basket.
She pulled out a nice long piece
of red thread.
"Thank you," Fred said.
He sat right down and sewed up
the cat's pajamas.

Fred and Red started home.
On the way, Fred put down
the cat's pajamas
so he could tie his shoe.

Along came a great big dog
and ran off with the cat's pajamas.
"Stop! Stop!" Fred called.
"You are running away with
the cat's pajamas."

The great big dog leaped over a hedge.
Red leaped over the hedge after him.
Fred ran around the edge of the hedge.

By the time Fred and Red
caught up with the great big dog
running away with the cat's pajamas,
a tall boy had taken them from the dog
and tied them to his kite.

All Fred and Red could do
was stand there
gazing up into the sky,
watching the cat's pajamas
flying higher and higher.

"Doesn't that piece of red cloth with
white flowers look nice as the tail
of my kite?" the tall boy asked Fred.

"Those are the cat's pajamas," Fred said.
"I just made them today."
"Oh," the tall boy said. "I didn't know."

Hand over hand he began bringing down
the kite so he could return the cat's pajamas.
But the kite got caught in the top of a tree.
"Don't worry," the tall boy said.
"I can climb that tree."

So the tall boy climbed the tree,
untied the cat's pajamas,
and tossed them down to Fred—
just as a garbage truck
was passing underneath.
The cat's pajamas fell into the
garbage in the back of the truck.

Fred and Red ran after the truck.
Fred was shouting and pointing.
"What's the matter?"
shouted the driver, slowing down.
"You're driving away with
the cat's pajamas," Fred said.

The driver stopped the truck.
With two fingers he picked
the cat's pajamas out of the garbage
and gave them to Fred.
"Thank you," Fred said.
He held the cat's pajamas far
from his nose as he walked away.

A girl was coming toward Fred and Red.
She made a face at them and said,
"You'd better not get that
dirty old rag near me."

"This is not a dirty old rag," Fred said.
"These are the cat's pajamas.
I am taking them home to wash
and dry them."

When Fred and Red got home,
Fred washed and dried the cat's pajamas.
Then he looked for the cat.
She wasn't in the garage.
She wasn't asleep in the chair next door.
She wasn't on the window sill.

But she WAS curled up fast asleep
in the basket right in the laundry room.
The cat took one look at the pajamas,
hissed, and ran away.

"Now what will I do with cat's pajamas?"
Fred said. He looked at Red.
"Would you like to try on the cat's pajamas?"
"Narf, narf," Red said.
Fred scratched his head.
"I have an idea," he said.

He stuffed the cat's pajamas
with lots of soft cotton,
sewed up the ends,
and put them on the sofa
for a fine new pillow.

That's what happened to the cat's pajamas.
Thank you.

Notes to Grown-ups

Major Themes

Here is a quick guide to the significant themes and concepts at work in *The Cat's Pajamas*:

- Staying with it: Fred did not give up in spite of all the difficulties.
- Making the best of things: as Fred did at the end when he found an alternative use for the cloth.
- Doing something for others: Fred was doing something he thought the cat would like.

Step-by-step Ideas for Reading and Talking

Here are some ideas for further give-and-take between grown-ups and children. The following topics encourage creative discussion of *The Cat's Pajamas* and invite the kind of open-ended response that is consistent with many contemporary approaches to reading, including Whole Language:

- Logical thinking: why did Fred give up asking for thread from the woman with all the children?

- Listening to rhyme and alliteration is good pre-reading training. Examples from this story include: Fred and Red, red thread, the edge of the hedge, and Fred said.

- What may have happened to Mr. May?

- There seems to be a lot of red cloth left over. What do you suppose Fred did with it?

Games for Learning

Games and activities can stimulate young readers and listeners alike to find out more about words, numbers, and ideas. Here are more ideas for turning learning into fun:

Cat's Pajamas Gift Wrap

Your child can make attractive wrapping paper that resembles the lively fabric of the cat's pajamas. For this activity, you will need a potato, a paring knife, white tempera paint, and red crepe paper.

Cut a potato in half for your child. Using a paring knife, carefully cut a simple elevated flower shape into the potato half. Then show your child how to dip the potato into a small amount of white tempera paint and use it as a stamp to make designs in the crepe paper. Let the paper dry completely, and then use it to wrap gifts.

You can also use commercially prepared stamps for making your gift wrap.

The Kitten's Mittens

Make a pattern for a tiny mitten, approximately 1 inch x 2 inches (2.5 centimeters x 5 centimeters), on an index card and cut out the design. Have your child trace the pattern two times on a piece of colorful felt. Cut out the mitten outlines for your child. Apply glue to one side of the outline of one of the mittens, except for the base of the mitten. Carefully place the second mitten on top, gluing the two together but leaving the base open. Stick the mittens onto one prong of a flat hair clip. Use your "kitten's mitten" as a bookmark or barrette.

About the Author

Raised in the Ozark Mountains, IDA CHITTUM came to children's book writing with a background steeped in the storytelling tradition of that area. When her own children were grown, she extended the fun she had telling stories to the written word. Over the last ten years, she has published an equal number of books. *The Cat's Pajamas*, her eleventh, is her first for Parents.

Ida Chittum and her husband divide their time between southern California and Illinois, where she still does a lot of storytelling to groups of various ages.

About the Artist

Before turning to children's book illustration, ART CUMINGS worked in film. There he developed a keen sense of how to make a story move visually, which he brought with him to his book projects.

In addition to his illustrations for other children's publishers, Mr. Cumings is now a Parents regular, with two other Parents books to his credit: *Septimus Bean and His Amazing Machine* (by Janet Quin-Harkin) and *A Good Fish Dinner* (by Barbara K. Walker).

The Cumings family lives in Douglaston, New York.